Dodgeball, Drama, and other Dilemmas

by Michele Jakubowski ★ illustrated by Luisa Montalto

PICTURE WINDOW BOOKS
a capstone imprint

Sidney & Sydney is published by Picture Window Books
A Capstone Imprint
1710 Roe Crest Drive
North Mankato, Minnesota 56003
www.capstonepub.com

Library of Congress Cataloging-in-Publication Data
Jakubowski, Michele.
 Sidney & Sydney : dodgeball, drama, and other dilemmas / by Michele
Jakubowski ; illustrated by Luisa Montalto.
    p. cm. -- (Sidney & Sydney ; bk. 2)
 Summary: Eight-year-olds Sydney (girl) and Sidney (boy) are neighbors,
classmates, and usually friends, so working together on the school play
should not be too difficult.
ISBN 978-1-4048-8061-0 (library binding)
ISBN 978-1-4795-2116-6 (paper over board)
1. Friendship--Juvenile fiction. 2. Children's plays--Juvenile fiction.
3. Elementary schools--Juvenile fiction. [1. Friendship--Fiction. 2.
Theater--Fiction. 3. Elementary schools--Fiction. 4. Schools--Fiction.]
I. Montalto, Luisa, ill. II. Title. III. Title: Sidney and Sydney. IV. Title:
Dodgeball, drama, and other dilemmas.
 PZ7.J153556Shm 2013
 813.6--dc23   2012049363

Design: Kay Fraser

Printed in China.
032013
007228RRDF13

FOR JOHN. XOXO
—M.J.

TABLE OF CONTENTS

Name: Sydney Shelby Baxter Greene
Age: 8
Birthdate: August 3
Parents: Bob and Jane Greene
Siblings: Owen (my baby brother)
Hobbies: fashion, playing *Galaxy Conquest*, reading

Sydney and best friend Harley

Sydney Greene

is a sassy third grader. Not only does she love fashion, but she loves a good game of *Galaxy Conquest* as well. She might be the smallest kid in the class, but she's also the spunkiest! Her best friend is Harley Livingston, a third-grade soccer star. They have been best friends since preschool, when Harley kicked a soccer ball into Sydney's face.

Name: **Sidney Patrick Fletcher**

Age: 8

Birthdate: May 11

Parents: Paula Fletcher

Siblings: None

Hobbies: sports, playing *Galaxy Conquest*, telling jokes

Sidney and best friend Gomez

Sidney Fletcher

is a quiet kid who loves sports. He is also the newest third grader in Oak Grove. However, it didn't take him long to make friends. Gomez (whose real name is Marco Xavier Gomez) is Sidney's first and best friend in Oak Grove. With one joke at the bus stop, Sidney and Gomez became inseparable.

CHAPTER 1

Cursive Writing and Spelling Bees

Sometimes I wish I had a different name. And it's not because my friend Sidney has the same name and he's a boy. That did bother me at the beginning of the year, but not anymore. I wish my name were different because we're finally learning how to write cursive.

I thought it was going to be fun and make everything look extra fancy. Instead it was hard and annoying. The capital "S" is almost impossible to write! The rest of the letters aren't very easy either.

I was still working on my cursive "S" when my third-grade teacher, Mr. Luther, said, "Put your notebooks and pencils away. I have an announcement to make."

I was glad because my hand was really starting to hurt. My head was starting to hurt, too.

"I have some very exciting news," Mr. Luther said. "On Friday we will be participating in Oak Grove Elementary's Third-Grade Spelling Bee!"

Mr. Luther looked around the room. I think he was waiting for us to be excited.

I knew I was a good speller. I also liked to play games, and I really liked to win! Maybe a spelling bee would be fun.

"I'll be sending home a list of words for you to study," Mr. Luther said. "We'll also spend some time each day in class practicing."

"Sounds like extra work to me," grumbled Nick.

We already had a lot more homework in third grade than we did in second. Now, on top of our math flash cards and worksheets, we were going to have extra spelling words. Maybe the spelling bee wouldn't be fun after all. Nobody likes extra work.

Gomez raised his hand. "Mr. Luther? Do we have to be in the spelling bee?"

Gomez was not the best speller, so I think he was nervous.

"Yes, Gomez," Mr. Luther said. "Our whole class will be participating. In fact, all of the third-grade classes will be participating. It will be fun for everyone."

I'm not sure Mr. Luther knows what kids like to do for fun. If he did, he wouldn't have said that spelling was fun.

The room was quiet. I looked around. No one seemed very happy about the spelling bee. Even my very best friend, Harley, looked worried. She's not the best speller, but she isn't terrible, either. Nobody looked as worried as Gomez.

Then Mr. Luther smiled and said, "Oh, I forgot the best part."

I sat up a little in my chair. So did everyone else.

Mr. Luther continued. "The winner of the spelling bee wins a gift card to Game On, the new video game store!"

Now everyone was really excited! Mr. Luther really should have said the part about the gift card first. I knew exactly what I would buy with that gift card. I would buy the new *Galaxy Conquest* video game. *Galaxy Conquest* is my favorite game of all time. I wanted to have *Galaxy Conquest 2* more than anything!

Maybe I'd never be able to make a perfect "S" in cursive, but I was going to win that spelling bee.

CHAPTER 2

Sidney the Super Speller

"I heard that in *Galaxy Conquest 2* there is a secret way around a player's force field," I said.

Sydney and I were up in my room hanging out. You might think it's weird that I was hanging out with a girl, but Sydney is cool. Our moms are best friends, so we end up spending a lot of time together.

Besides, Gomez was busy with music lessons and Harley was busy with swim team, so we both needed something to do.

That night, our moms were downstairs with the rest of their book club. My mom didn't want me to get bored, so she asked Mrs. Greene to bring Sydney.

We had just snuck downstairs to get more delicious snacks. I don't know much about book clubs, but I do know that they are very loud, and there is always a lot of good food. I'm not even sure that they really read any books.

Sydney finished up her chocolate chip cookie. She wiped the crumbs off her hands as she said, "I know! And I heard that the supersonic power star is now worth triple points!"

"Really?" I asked. "Wow! That could

change the whole game. I can't wait to
play it!"

Ever since Sydney got to my house that
night, we had been talking about the new
Galaxy Conquest 2 video game. We were
beyond excited about the new version!

"It's a good thing I'm such a good
speller," I told Sydney.

"You are?" she asked.

"At my old school, I was the best speller
in my class. Everyone called me Sidney
the Super Speller," I explained. "I'm sure
I'll win the spelling bee. Then I'll use the
money to buy *Galaxy Conquest 2*. We can
play it together. "

When Mr. Luther told us about the spelling bee, I was excited. The rest of the kids didn't like that we had extra homework. They also didn't like that instead of read-aloud time we were going to be working on spelling.

I didn't mind. I was already a good speller, so I didn't need to practice at home. And the read-aloud book we were listening to was not my favorite. It was about a little girl who lives on a farm. Her horse is sick, and she's trying to get her parents to let her keep it.

Everybody else in my class loved that book. Some of the kids even cried a little while listening. I thought it was boring.

As we walked into the living room, I looked at Sydney. She had that look on her face that she gets when I win a game. It wasn't a happy look. It was a look that I wasn't going to mess with.

"I'm a really good speller, too," she said. "In fact, people should call ME Sydney the Super Speller."

"Ummm...okay," I said quietly. "Good night."

"Whatever," she said.

And that's how we ended our night.

CHAPTER 3

I Meant the Other Sidney

Not only am I a good speller, but I'm a rock star in gym class. I don't want to brag, but it's true. Besides art, gym is my favorite class. It might be surprising since I'm so small, but it doesn't matter. I'm quick and strong.

The day after we found out about the spelling bee, I was really looking forward to gym class. I needed a break from spelling, and exercising always made me feel better.

The best thing about gym is our teacher, Mr. Panino. He says he has been teaching at Oak Grove Elementary School his whole life. If that is true, he's been teaching there a long time.

I'm not sure how old Mr. Panino is, but he has gray hair like my grandpa. He also likes to tell stories about the good old days. None of us ever know what he's talking about, but it doesn't matter. Mr. Panino is the greatest gym teacher ever!

We sat down in a row on the gym floor. Mr. Panino said, "Class, today we are going to play dodgeball."

Yes! Of all the fun things we do in gym, dodgeball is my favorite! Every time we choose teams for dodgeball, I am picked first. Since the first time we played dodgeball in kindergarten, I have either been the captain or the first one picked.

Also, dodgeball is a great way to relieve stress. And ever since Mr. Luther told us about the spelling bee, I was feeling pretty stressed out.

"Gomez and Alexa, you two can be team captains," Mr. Panino said.

The captains stood in front of the class. Mr. Panino took out the quarter he always uses to decide who will pick first. Mr. Panino is very fair.

Alexa picked heads, and it was tails. Doesn't Alexa know that tails never fails?

I better tell her that for future games. I was happy, though, because Gomez knew how good I was at dodgeball. I was sure he would pick me first.

I would rather be captain, but being the first one picked meant I could help the captain get the best team.

I looked around at our class. I was trying to decide whom Gomez should pick after me. Nick was good, but he didn't always play fair. Aubrey was really good, too, but she had a sprained ankle.

I saw Sidney sitting at the end of the row. He was new to the school this year, so we'd never seen him play dodgeball before. But I liked hanging out with him, and we had become good friends. I decided to be nice and have Gomez pick Sidney after me.

As Gomez called my name, I began to stand up. I was about halfway up when I heard him say something else.

"Ummm...I meant the other Sidney," he said quietly.

I heard Nick laugh, and I felt my cheeks get hot. I couldn't believe I wasn't picked first!

Alexa picked me first for her team, but I was still mad and embarrassed. The first dodgeball game of the year was off to a terrible start.

CHAPTER 4

The Dodgeball Queen

Mr. Panino is an awesome gym teacher. He must be a million years old, because he taught at Oak Grove Elementary when my mom went to school!

I was excited when Mr. Panino said that we were playing dodgeball. Not to brag or anything, but I'm pretty good at dodgeball. I guess Gomez knew that, because he picked me first for his team.

As we got ready to play, I was surprised to hear the other players on my team saying things like, "Watch out for Sydney!" or, "Let's try to knock out Sydney first."

I was so confused. "Sydney Greene?" I asked Gomez.

I knew that she was a great *Galaxy Conquest* player, but she was super small. How good could she be at dodgeball?

"Oh, yeah," Gomez said, "she's the dodgeball queen. If I didn't pick you first, I would have definitely picked her. But you are my best friend, so I thought I should pick you."

I kept my eye on Sydney the whole time. Not only was she fast, but she was strong. She could really throw the ball! Soon the only players left were me, Nathan, and Gomez on my side and Sydney and Ryan on the other side.

As I ran to the back of the gym to get a ball, I watched Sydney. I saw her catch the ball Gomez had thrown at her. In a flash, she threw it and hit Nathan. In a matter of seconds, she had taken out two players. I was the only one left on my team.

I quickly grabbed a ball and threw it as hard as I could. Sydney was able to dodge it, but I hit Ryan on the arm. The game was down to me and Sydney.

Neither of us had a ball in reach. We stood there for a long time, staring at each other. I knew what I had to do. I had to pull out my signature dodgeball move. A move that worked every time. A move that would make Sydney really mad, but it didn't matter. I had to win this game.

I faked to my right, then dove to my left and grabbed a ball from the ground. My fake worked and Sydney moved the other way. She was trapped. Not a single ball was in her reach. I wound my arm back ready to win the game.

Next thing I knew, Mr. Panino was blowing his whistle. "Good game, but we're out of time."

"What?!" Sydney and I both shouted at the same time.

"That's not fair!" I protested. "I was just about to get her out!"

"You were not," Sydney said, crossing her arms. "I was ready for you! I was going to catch that ball and get you out!"

"No way!" I said, taking a step toward her.

"Yes way!" she replied, stepping toward me. She got up on her tiptoes, and we were almost face to face.

Mr. Panino stepped between us and
said, "That's enough! It's just a game."

It was more than a game, and both
of us knew it. If I couldn't be the official
winner of the dodgeball game, I was
definitely going to win that spelling bee!

CHAPTER 5

Done.
D-O-N-E.

Sidney and I hadn't talked since the day
of the dodgeball game. Four days is a long
time to go without talking to someone. But
I stayed busy.

To get ready for the spelling bee, I
practiced my words after school each day.
I also walked around the house spelling
things that I saw. "Table, t-a-b-l-e. Chair,
c-h-a-i-r. Owen, O-w-e-n. Mess, m-e-s-s."

The day of the spelling bee finally arrived. I was nervous. The whole third grade was on the stage. We had to draw numbers to see what order we would go in. I was number one.

I looked into the crowd and saw my
mom and dad. My mom was sitting next
to Sidney's mom, Mrs. Fletcher. I really
liked Mrs. Fletcher, but seeing her made
me mad at Sidney all over again.

Mr. Luther stood up and thanked all the
parents for coming. He told everyone how

the spelling bee worked, but I didn't listen. I already knew how this thing would work. It would start with me spelling words correctly and end with me winning.

Finally Mr. Luther called for speller number one to go to the microphone. That was me! I was happy to go first and show everyone my spelling skills. Maybe it would even make Sidney nervous.

I liked having everyone's attention. It felt good to stand at the microphone and smile at all the people. I felt like a movie star! I waved a little to my parents. I had worn my favorite outfit and was ready to win this thing!

I looked down at the table in front of the stage. Mr. Luther was sitting there with

another third-grade teacher, Mrs. Madden, and the school principal, Mrs. Denny. They were all smiling at me. This was going to be a piece of cake!

"Are you ready, Sydney?" Mr. Luther asked.

"Yes!" I said, too loudly. The microphone made an awful squeaking sound. How embarrassing!

Everyone in the audience put their hands over their ears. I could hear kids giggling behind me. I felt my cheeks get warm. I wasn't feeling quite so confident anymore.

Mrs. Denny asked me to take a step back. Then I took a deep breath to relax.

"Is that better?" I said in a much softer voice.

"Yes," Mrs. Madden said. "Your first word, Sydney, is 'cucumber.'"

I smiled. We'd had salad with our dinner the night before, and I had practiced all the words — lettuce, carrot, tomato, and cucumber. I was going to get this right for sure!

I felt one step closer to winning the gift card to the new video game store. Then I could buy *Galaxy Conquest 2* and brag to Sidney about it.

I smiled and quickly said, "Cucumber. C-u-c-m-b-e-r. Cucumber."

I was headed back to my chair when I heard a buzzer and Mr. Luther say, "I'm sorry, Sydney. That's not correct."

I spun around so quickly my pink skirt twirled. "What?" I asked.

"'Cucumber' is c-u-c-u-m-b-e-r,'" Mrs. Madden said. "You missed the second 'u.'"

I couldn't believe what I was hearing! Not only was I not going to win the spelling bee, but I was done on the first word! This was beyond embarrassing.

I was done. D-o-n-e. Done.

CHAPTER 6

And the Winner Is...

After some very tough rounds, the spelling bee was down to me and Gomez. I knew I was a good speller, but Gomez was surprising everyone. Including himself!

Sydney went out on the first word. She had spelled her word too fast. She didn't stop to think about it. I knew I couldn't make that mistake.

Mr. Luther had told us that the spelling bee was not a race, so I took my time on each word.

Gomez had not been excited about the spelling bee. He had a tough time with spelling. But he was a hard worker, and he'd been practicing his words every night.

I knew this because every day I asked him to play, and he wouldn't. He wanted to study instead. I thought it was lame at the time, but as I heard my next word, I knew Gomez was smart to study. I really should have studied, too.

"Your word is 'theory,'" Mr. Luther said.

I thought about it for a little bit and said, "Theory, t-h-e-e-r-y, theory."

I could tell by the looks on the judges' faces that I'd gotten it wrong.

"I'm sorry, Sidney, that is incorrect," Mrs. Madden said.

And just like that, I was done. No gift card for me. Now I would never get to play the new *Galaxy Conquest* game.

As I was sitting in my chair feeling sorry for myself, I heard Gomez spell his final word right.

"And the winner of this year's spelling bee is Gomez!" Mr. Luther announced.

I couldn't believe it! Gomez's last word was "insulin," which is kind of funny because Gomez is diabetic. He uses insulin to keep his blood sugar at the right level. He's probably known how to spell that word since kindergarten!

I was happy for Gomez, but I still felt angry about losing. I really wanted to win! I was mad at myself for not practicing more. I had been so sure that I would win. I guess being sure isn't the same as being prepared.

Afterward, everyone congratulated Gomez. He seemed so happy. I felt sort of bad for feeling angry. But then again, how was I supposed to feel happy? I lost.

Gomez walked over to me.

"Congratulations," I said. "You were awesome." I tried to smile at him, but my face just couldn't do it. Instead, it just twitched a little and looked weird.

"What's wrong with your face?" Gomez asked. He wasn't having any trouble smiling.

"Nothing. Nothing at all," I said. I tried to make my face look normal.

Then Gomez did something shocking. Something so shocking that it made my face go all weird again.

"I want you to have this," he said. And he reached out and handed me the gift card to Game On.

"What?" I asked. I couldn't believe it! "But you worked so hard to win it! Why would you want to give it to me?"

"I worked hard because I wanted to win," Gomez said.

"I know," I said. "But I can't take this from you."

"You know I don't really like video games. Plus, my parents promised to take me to Super Fun Adventureland if I won. That was all the motivation I needed," Gomez said with a smile.

"But you earned this, too," I said.

"I did," he said. "And now I'm giving it to you. What good is winning if you can't celebrate with your friend?"

I wasn't having any trouble smiling now. I looked around for Sydney and couldn't find her. Then my smile started to fade, and my face felt weird again.

CHAPTER 7

Great Minds Think Alike

What a horrible week! First there was that awful dodgeball game. Then I went out of the spelling bee on the first word. And now, on Saturday, it was raining so I couldn't play outside.

I heard my mom calling me. "Sydney! Someone is here for you!"

I jumped off my bed. Maybe Harley had come to cheer me up! I ran downstairs, excited to see my best friend. Instead, I saw Sidney.

"What do you want?" I asked with complete annoyance.

"I wanted to show you this," he said, proudly holding up the new *Galaxy Conquest* video game.

Wow! *Galaxy Conquest 2*! I tried to stay calm and act like I didn't care, but it was hard.

"Where did you get that?" I asked.

"Gomez gave me the gift card to Game On, and I went and bought it right away," he said. "It turns out Gomez wasn't kidding when he said he didn't like video games."

I couldn't contain my excitement anymore.

"That's just crazy! How could someone
not like *Galaxy Conquest*?" I asked.

"I know!" Sidney agreed. "So, do you
want to play?"

We both stood there for a few seconds. I
was still mad about the dodgeball game, but
I really wanted to play *Galaxy Conquest 2*.

"Do you really have to ask?" I said with
a smile.

"Awesome," Sidney said.

We were just about to go downstairs
when Sidney said, "I guess you probably
could have caught that ball and got me
out."

"You never know," I said. "You throw

really hard. You could have aimed for my legs and got me out."

Suddenly Sidney had a big smile on his face. "Hey, I've got an idea! Next time let's try to get on the same team!"

"Nobody could beat us!" I agreed.

We headed to the basement and started our game of *Galaxy Conquest 2*. It was even better than we had hoped!

Sidney was winning most of the game, but in the end I used my superhuman power shield and won.

At first, Sidney looked mad. Then he said, "Good game."

"You, too," I said.

"Let's go celebrate your first win in *Galaxy Conquest 2*," Sidney said.

"With ice cream?" I asked.

"Duh!" Sidney said.

"Perfect! What good is winning if you can't celebrate with your friend?" I said.

"That's exactly what Gomez told me," Sidney replied.

"Great minds think alike," I said. "Now let's go get that ice cream!"

CHAPTER 8

What's the Worst That Could Happen?

Sydney and I spent the whole weekend playing my new *Galaxy Conquest 2* game. So on Monday, I really wished I could have brought the game to school. I especially wished that once Mr. Luther told us we'd be having indoor recess. He said it was too cold to go outside.

I hated indoor recess. It was so boring! I was ready to go outside and play. Plus, we had been planning a basketball tournament at recess. I had even written down the teams and planned out the games on a piece of paper. Now we were going to be stuck inside.

Gomez and I sat on the floor, trying to find all the pieces to the checkers game. I looked up when Mrs. Dover, one of the fifth-grade teachers, came into the room.

"Hello, Mr. Luther's class!" she called. Mrs. Dover is what my mom would call a very chipper person. When she talked, it almost sounded like she was singing.

"I wanted to talk to you all about something very exciting happening at Oak Grove Elementary!" Mrs. Dover went on. "As those of you with older brothers or sisters might know, every year the school puts on a play. Usually we only allow the fourth and fifth graders to be in it, but this year we are opening the auditions to the third graders as well!"

After losing the spelling bee, I was not that interested in getting back up on the stage, so I went back to looking for all the missing checker pieces.

"Rehearsals will be during recess time," Mr. Luther said. "And those of you who participate will get extra credit toward your reading grades."

This got my attention. I had fallen behind a little in reading. My mom had said that if I didn't get my grade up, I couldn't join the basketball team.

"Can't be worse than playing checkers without all the pieces," Gomez whispered.

"My mom said it's going to be a cold winter, so I bet we'll be stuck inside a lot," I said.

"Do you want to try out for the play?" Gomez asked.

"Sure, why not?" I said. "What's the worst that could happen?"

CHAPTER 9

Look Out, Hollywood!

I love being in the spotlight and having all eyes on me. I had really loved being onstage during the spelling bee — until I lost, of course. I only wished I could have been up there longer! The school play would be a great way to get onstage again.

Harley and I decided to try out for the school play together. Mrs. Dover had written the play. It was about a man named Mr. Jones and his daughter, Jane.

Mrs. Dover wanted the fourth and fifth graders to play the adults. I could see why Mrs. Dover would do that. Some of those fourth and fifth graders were huge!

I heard some of the older kids talking. They said that the only reason the third graders got to try out is because Mrs. Dover needed smaller kids to play Jane's friends.

I didn't really care what the reason was. I just cared about getting on that stage again!

Harley and I were trying out for parts as Jane's friends. We wouldn't have to say anything during the play. There was a lot of singing and dancing, and I liked that.

Mrs. Dover put us into groups of four. We had to sing part of a song and do a

little dance. I thought the dance was easy,
but some girls had trouble. Harley was
nervous, but I wasn't at all.

About halfway through our tryout, Mrs. Dover stopped us and pointed at me. "What's your name, sweetie?" she asked.

"Sydney Greene," I told her. I thought I was doing a good job, but I must have messed up. My cheeks turned bright red. I probably looked like a tomato.

"Are you really in third grade?" she asked.

I felt my cheeks get ever more red. I was the smallest kid in my class. She must have thought I was a second grader. How embarrassing!

"Yes," I mumbled.

Mrs. Dover smiled. "Would you mind singing a little by yourself?"

"I would love to!" I said, no longer embarrassed. This was my big chance!

I sang the whole song and did the dance, too. When I was done, Mrs. Dover stood up and clapped. So did all the other kids in the auditorium.

"That was wonderful, Sydney!" she said. "Ben, please stand next to Sydney."

A fifth grade boy walked over and stood next to me. He was really tall. I had to tilt my head all the way back to look up at him. The top of my head didn't even make it to his shoulder!

Mrs. Dover clapped her hands to get everyone's attention. "Everyone, listen up!" she called. "I'd like you all to meet the

stars of our play! Ben will be playing Mr. Jones, and Sydney will be Jane. Great job, you two!"

I couldn't believe it! I had been hoping for a small part in the play, and I got the lead role!

I couldn't stop smiling as everyone clapped for us. People were cheering for me! I could get used to that. Look out, Hollywood! Here comes Sydney Greene!

CHAPTER 10

Under What?

As soon as Gomez and I walked into the play tryouts, we knew we had made a mistake.

The girls were trying out first. I saw Sydney singing and dancing on the stage by herself. She was really good!

"We have to sing and dance?" I asked Gomez. "By ourselves?"

I didn't want to sing and dance in a group, and I really didn't want to do it alone!

"I didn't know there was singing!" Gomez said. "Or dancing!"

He looked just as worried as I did. I guess neither of us had been paying attention when Mrs. Dover said that the play was a musical. If we had heard that part, we definitely wouldn't be in this position right now.

We turned around to leave and bumped right into Mr. Luther.

"Hello, boys! I'm glad to see you here," Mr. Luther said. "I was just talking with

your mom about your reading grade,
Sidney. Participating in the play is just the
boost you'll need to pick that grade up!"

Now I was stuck. I really wanted to play basketball, and the only way my mom was going to let me join the team was if I got my reading grade up.

"I was just here to wish Sidney luck," Gomez said quickly.

"That was nice of you," Mr. Luther smiled.

"Yep, well, that's the kind of friend I am!" Gomez said. He started walking toward the door and added, "Good luck, Sidney! Break a leg or whatever it is they say."

Before I could say anything, he was gone. I couldn't believe it! My best friend had left me!

Right after Gomez left, Mrs. Dover announced that Sydney and some fifth grade boy named Ben were going to be the stars in the play.

I was happy for Sydney, and I'm sure she was thrilled. I know how much she loves to be front and center. However, I still wasn't so sure about being in a play, let alone a musical!

"The last group to try out is the third grade boys," Mrs. Dover said. "There is no dancing in these roles, but you will be doing a little singing."

If I had to choose between singing and dancing, I would for sure pick singing. Maybe I could do this.

There were only six third grade boys. I stood at the end of the line.

Mrs. Dover looked up at us. When she saw me she said, "This is for third grade boys. The fourth and fifth grade boys already tried out."

I was tall for my age, so I guess she thought I was older. That happened to me a lot.

"I am in third grade," I told her. Maybe I was too tall for the play. Mr. Luther would have to give me the extra credit for trying, right?

"Hmmm," Mrs. Dover said. She looked like she was thinking really hard. "Can you sing?"

"I guess," I said.

"Do you think you could sing part of the song right now?" she ask.

"I could try," I said.

She gave me the sheet music and cued the piano player. At first I felt embarrassed, but when I noticed that no one was laughing, I felt better. I kept singing and singing and singing.

Before I knew it, I had sung the entire song. All the kids in the auditorium started clapping. I was feeling pretty good about myself. I guess I know why Sydney likes being on the stage now. I smiled, took a bow, and climbed off the stage.

Before I could get very far, Mrs. Dover stopped me.

"You are very good," she said. "I think we just found Ben's understudy."

"Under what?" I asked.

"Understudy means that you will fill in for Ben if he can't perform," she explained. "You two look alike and are almost the same size for the costume."

I got a big smile on my face. "So, if Ben can perform, I don't have to?"

"That's right. You will need to learn his part and practice, but if he is able to, he will perform the role in the play," Mrs. Dover said.

"And I still get credit for reading?" I asked Mr. Luther.

Mr. Luther laughed. "Yes, Sidney."

"Perfect!" I said. Now I could play basketball — and I wouldn't have to sing or dance!

CHAPTER 11

Unhelpful Advice

After one week, I was still convinced that being in the play was great. Since I was one of the stars, I got to miss part of math every afternoon. I felt very special leaving class and walking down to the fifth grade hallway.

The rest of the time, though, we practiced during recess. Those practices were the hardest because the other third grade girls in the play weren't doing so well. They had complained all week about rehearsals being too hard. I was a little tired of it.

"Okay, everyone, take five," Mrs. Dover said during one recess rehearsal.

"Take five" is the way people in plays say "take a break." I think that is so cool!

My friends and I walked down the hall and gathered around the drinking fountain.

"The final dance scene is so hard!" said Taylor.

"I know!" Harley agreed. "I feel like we practice and practice, but I just can't get it right!"

In the scene where the others were dancing, I was standing behind them on the stage. I could tell they were all having a hard time with it.

"It looks like you all keep tripping over each other," I told them. I didn't want to sound mean, but it was the truth.

Taylor crossed her arms and said, "I've been taking dance lessons for five years, and this is the hardest dance I've ever done in my life."

"I think if Taylor and Josie remembered to go right and Harley and Ayesha went left, you wouldn't keep bumping into each other," I said.

I had the best view of them dancing, so
I felt like I had the best advice.

"It's not as easy as it looks," Ayesha
snapped at me.

"I didn't say it looked easy," I told her, frowning. "I was just trying to give you some helpful advice."

Harley nodded and said, "You just don't understand because you don't have to do this dance."

"Just because you are the star of the play doesn't mean you know everything," Ayesha said.

"We don't need your unhelpful advice," Taylor said.

All of my friends were ganging up on me! Totally unfair! I was only trying to help them.

"I may not know about this dance, but

I've got it even harder. Try learning ten pages of lines!" I said.

My voice squeaked a little and I thought I might start to cry.

"Plus I have to do three dances and learn five new songs!" I said with a big sigh.

I was upset, so I took a long drink of water to calm down. When I finished my drink I saw that the three of them were halfway down the hall. They had all left without me.

CHAPTER 12

No More Understudy

Being an understudy was a piece of
cake! Rehearsals were easy. I spent most
of the time watching what Ben was doing.
Sometimes I snuck a book or a sports
magazine in and read instead.

I had been doing better in reading and
with the extra credit from the play my
mom was sure to let me join the basketball
team.

I knew Mr. Luther would be glad if I made the team. He was a big sports fan. He even taped a big football field across the top of the board in our classroom. Every time our class got a compliment from another teacher or had a good day, he moved a little player down the field. Once the player made it all the way across the field, we'd get to have a movie party.

And not just a boring school movie, but a real movie, like the ones you see in the theater. We'd even get to have popcorn!

We were about halfway down the field, so Mr. Luther said we could celebrate with an extra recess. The only problem was that it was super cold out again.

"Oh, great, indoor recess again," I said to Gomez. "I wish we could have saved the extra recess for when we can play outside."

"Indoor recess is fun now," Gomez said.

"It is?" I asked. I had been at play practice during recess for the past few weeks. Part of the reason I joined the play was to get away from boring indoor recess!

"Oh, yeah!" Gomez said. "A couple of weeks ago Nathan showed us how to play this great game. It's called paper football. See?" Gomez held up a piece of paper that had been folded up into a triangle.

"What's that?" I asked. It sure didn't look like a football to me!

"Watch," Gomez said. He waved Nathan over. "Let's show Sidney how to play."

Gomez put his thumbs together and held up his pointer fingers. They made a "u" shape that looked like a goal post. Nathan put one corner of the paper triangle on the table and held it still using his finger. With his other hand, he flicked the triangle across the table and through Gomez's hands.

"Score!" Gomez shouted.

"That is so cool!" I told them.

"We've been having tournaments and keeping track of the winners," Gomez said.

He pulled out a notebook that had all the scores and winners listed in it. I can't believe I had been missing out on all the fun for a dumb play!

I watched as the other kids played. It was almost my turn when I saw Mrs. Dover race into our room.

"Is Sidney Fletcher in here?" she asked Mr. Luther.

"I'm right here," I said.

"Are you feeling all right?" Mrs. Dover asked.

"Uh...I guess so," I answered.

"Thank goodness!" she said again. "Ben has come down with the flu and will be out for a few days. You're going to have to take his place in the play. You are no longer the understudy. You are the lead!"

My stomach flipped. Maybe I wasn't feeling so well after all!

CHAPTER 13

Flowers and Friendship

It was the night of the play, and instead of being happy, I felt awful. Since Ben got sick, we had been practicing twice a day and after school. Sidney was doing really well, but I could tell he was nervous.

I had been so busy practicing with Sidney that I hadn't seen Harley and the other girls at all. I was still upset about what had happened in the hallway.

I felt like the other girls didn't understand how hard I was working. But I guess I didn't have to be so mean about it. They were working really hard, too.

My mom told me to apologize, but I wasn't sure a simple apology would be enough. What a mess!

I knew the rest of the cast was getting ready in the big room behind the stage. I could hear them talking and laughing.

I was sitting in my own dressing room. I should have felt extra special, but instead I felt sad and lonely.

I was checking my makeup in the mirror when I heard a voice behind me.

"Knock, knock!"

I turned around and saw Harley standing in the doorway. She was holding a bunch of flowers.

"What are those for?" I asked.

"To wish you good luck, silly!" Harley laughed. "I thought you knew all about the theater. My mom said it's a tradition to give an actor flowers on opening night."

I knew that opening night meant the first night a play was performed. I hadn't heard about the flowers part. I liked that tradition! It seemed so much nicer than telling someone to break a leg!

"You are the best friend in the whole world!" I said. "I was so worried that you were mad at me."

"I was a little mad," she said. "But I'm over it."

"I didn't mean to be so rude to everyone," I said. "I was just crabby and tired. I'm sorry."

"We were all crabby. I had no idea that being in a play was so much work!" Harley said.

"It sure is," I agreed. "Are the other girls still mad?"

"A little, but nothing an apology won't fix," Harley said. "And maybe some ice cream after the show."

"That sounds perfect!" I said.

Just then, Mrs. Dover knocked on the door. "Let's go, girls," she said. "It's almost showtime!"

Harley gave me a big hug. "Break a leg!" she said.

"You, too," I whispered back.

"And remember, no matter what happens out there, I'm proud of you," Mrs. Dover said.

"Thanks," I said.

I was proud of me, too.

CHAPTER 14

An Incredible Team

The play went perfectly. Well, almost perfectly. I did forget a few lines, but it didn't matter. The audience laughed and cried and cheered. And at the very end, they gave us a standing ovation.

As we walked offstage at the end of the play, Sydney gave me a big hug. I don't normally like to hug people, but I was so happy I hugged her back.

"We did it!" she cheered.

All of a sudden, we were surrounded by the rest of the kids from the play. We high-fived and congratulated each other.

I saw Gomez as he walked through the crowd. When he got to me he said, "Good job! Can I get your autograph?"

I smiled and said, "It'll cost you five bucks."

"You were awesome!" Gomez said. "After I saw all the singing and dancing at the tryouts, I didn't even want to come to this play. But it was really good! You and Sydney were great!"

"Thanks," I said. "I'm glad it's over. I can't wait to play paper football during recess."

Gomez shook his head and said, "We don't play that anymore."

"What? Why not?" I asked.

"It got kind of boring," Gomez explained.

"Oh," I said. I was disappointed. Indoor recess had been fun while I was busy with the play. Now that I would be back in the classroom, recess was going to be boring again. Bummer.

Gomez smiled and said, "Nathan and I talked to Mr. Luther and Mr. Panino. They said that since there are no gym classes during our recess, we could play dodgeball in the gym during indoor recess. Isn't that cool?"

"Excellent!" I said.

Then I remembered something. "We have to make sure Sydney the dodgeball queen is on our team."

Just then, someone called my name. I turned around and saw my mom, Granny, and Grandpa heading my way.

I could tell from halfway across the room that my mom was crying. My mom cries about the weirdest things. I even saw her cry once while watching a commercial for greeting cards. So weird!

Granny gave me a big hug and kiss. I let her, because she's my granny. Grandpa gave me a pat on the back and said, "Well done, son."

Then it was Mom's turn. "Oh, Sidney," she said, giving me a huge hug. "You worked so hard, and you did an amazing job! I'm so proud of you!"

"Thanks," I said.

I was proud of me, too.

I'm not sure if we'll do another play together, but me and Sydney really do make an incredible team.

Who knows what we'll do together next?

Sidney & Sydney

FAVORITES

SCHOOL SUBJECT

Sydney: Art. Definitely art. And gym, especially when we play dodgeball.

Sidney: I guess recess. I mean lunch! Yep. I love lunch.

SONG

Sydney: I have so many favorite songs! Any song by Taylor Swift is awesome.

Sidney: "We Are the Champions" by Queen. It was my dad's favorite song, too.

HOBBIES

Sydney: Singing, dancing, playing soccer, and hanging out with my friends.

Sidney: Playing basketball, playing piano (I bet you didn't know that, huh?), and hanging out with my friends. Oh, yeah, and playing video games.

COLOR

Sydney: Purple, especially purple with glitter and sparkles!

Sidney: Green. Just plain green.

FOOD

Sydney: Cereal and ice cream.

Sidney: Pizza and ice cream.

SEASON

Sydney: Summer!

Sidney: Summer!

ABOUT THE AUTHOR

Raised in the Chicago suburb of Hoffman Estates, Michele Jakubowski has the teachers in her life to thank for her love of reading and writing. While writing has always been a passion for Michele, she believes it is the books she has read throughout the years, and the teachers who assigned them, that have made her the storyteller she is today. Michele lives in Powell, Ohio, with her husband, John, and their children, Jack and Mia.

ABOUT THE ILLUSTRATOR

Luisa Montalto followed a curved path to becoming an illustrator. She was first a dancer, then earned her doctorate degree in cinematography. She credits these experiences with giving her the energy and will to try harder. Finally, she went on to work with an independent comics magazine before becoming a professional illustrator in 2003.